W9-BKD-411

A KNOW-NOTHING HALLOWEEN

story by Michele Sobel Spirn
pictures by R. W. Alley

HarperTrophy®
An Imprint of HarperCollins Publishers

For Ethan Ellenberg and Anne Hoppe,

who helped bring the Know-Nothings to life,

and for Steve and Josh

—M.S.S.

For Galen, the newest pumpkin

in the nephew patch

—R.W.A.

HarperCollins®, 🖤®, Harper Trophy®, and I Can Read Book®
are trademarks of HarperCollins Publishers Inc.

A Know-Nothing Halloween
Text copyright © 2000 by Michele Sobel Spirn
Illustrations copyright © 2000 by R. W. Alley
Printed in the U.S.A. All rights reserved.
www.harperchildrens.com

Library of Congress Cataloging-in-Publication Data
Spirn, Michele Sobel.
    A know-nothing Halloween / story by Michele Sobel Spirn ; illustrations by R.W. Alley.
        p.   cm. (An I can read book)
    Summary: Four easily confused friends find their own way to celebrate Halloween.
    ISBN 0-06-028185-5— ISBN 0-06-028186-3 (lib. bdg.) — ISBN 0-06-444252-7 (pbk.)
    [1. Halloween—Fiction.   2. Humorous stories.]   I. Alley, R. W. (Robert W.), Ill.   II. Title.
III. Series.
PZ7.S78626 Kn   2000   98-036618
[E]—dc21   CIP
                                                                                                        AC
First Harper Trophy Edition, 2001
❖

CONTENTS

HALLOWEEN TRICKS

Once there were four friends

named Boris, Morris,

Doris, and Norris.

People called them Know-Nothings.

They didn't know much,

but they knew they were best friends.

One day Norris said,

"Look! Here is a note for us."

"It's from Doris," said Morris.

"I will read it," said Norris.

"Dear Friends,

Today is Halloween.

I have gone to get something.

I will be back soon.

Love, Doris."

"Good reading, Norris," said Boris.

"What do you think she is getting?"
asked Norris.

"I am hungry," said Morris.

"Maybe it is French fries."

8

"Do people eat French fries
on Halloween?" asked Boris.

"I don't think so," said Norris.

"What do people do on Halloween?"
asked Boris.

9

"They cut up pumpkins," said Norris.

"That's terrible," said Boris.

"Those poor helpless pumpkins."

"What else do they do?"

asked Morris.

"They have parties," said Norris.

"Do they invite the pumpkins?"

asked Boris.

"No. They bob for apples,"

said Norris.

"Let's do that," said Morris.

"Who will get the apples?"
asked Norris.

"Who will get Bob?" asked Morris.

"Who is Bob?" asked Boris.

"Maybe Bob will get the apples,"
said Morris.

"But we don't know Bob," said Norris.

"So we can't invite him
to our Halloween party."

"I wish Bob could come,"
said Boris.

"If Bob does not come,

the apples will not come,"

said Morris.

"We will have to do something else,"

said Norris.

"We could trick-or-treat."

"How do we do that?" asked Morris.

"We go to people's houses
and do tricks for them," said Norris.

"Then they give us treats."

"I don't know any tricks,"

said Boris.

"Maybe Floris knows some tricks,"

said Norris.

"Sit, Floris."

"I don't think Floris

knows that trick," said Morris.

16

"Roll over, Floris," said Norris.

"Floris does not know
that trick either," said Morris.

"Stand on four legs, Floris,"
said Norris.

"What a great trick,"

said Morris.

"Floris is such a clever dog,"

said Boris.

Morris, Boris, and Norris
took Floris out to get some
Halloween treats.

HIDING FROM HALLOWEEN

Morris rang a doorbell.

A woman came to the door.

"Trick or treat," said Norris.

"Here is our trick," said Boris.

"Stand on four legs, Floris."

"Arf! Arf!" said Floris.

"Floris, you are barking!"

said Boris.

"You have learned

a new trick!"

"What are you dressed as?"

asked the woman.

"I am dressed as Morris,"

said Morris.

"I am dressed as Boris,"

said Boris.

"I am dressed as Norris,"

said Norris.

24

"Arf!" said Floris.

"Floris wants me to tell you that she is dressed as Floris," said Boris.

"But who are Boris, Norris,

Morris, and Floris?" asked the woman.

"They are us," said Morris.

"We are they," said Boris.

"I must go," said the woman.

She gave Boris, Morris, and Norris
some candy.

Morris, Norris, Boris, and Floris
started walking to the next house.
"Boo!" said someone behind them.

"It's a ghost!" yelled Norris.

"Run! Run for your lives!"

Boris, Morris, Norris, and Floris

ran all the way home.

They ran up to Boris's room.

They crawled under the bed

as far as they could go.

"No more Halloween for me,"

said Morris.

"It's scary out there."

30

Morris, Boris, Norris, and Floris
stayed under the bed
and waited for Halloween
to end.

Clump!

Clump!

Clump!

"What's that?" asked Norris.

"I think the ghost is coming

to get us," said Morris.

"It's getting closer," said Boris.

"Close your eyes," said Norris.

"Maybe it will not see us."

"Boris," called a voice.

"The ghost wants you, Boris," said Norris.

"Morris! Norris!" the voice called.

"It wants all of us," said Boris.

"Shh! Maybe the ghost

will not find us," said Morris.

Then the voice said,

"Why are you under the bed?"

"That sounds like Doris,"

said Morris.

"Maybe it's a ghost

pretending to be Doris,"

said Norris.

"Is that you, Doris?"

asked Morris.

"I think so," said Doris.

"We have to make sure

you are not a ghost,"

said Norris.

"Pinch yourself."

"Ow!" yelled Doris.

"It's really Doris," said Norris.

"A pinch would not hurt a ghost."

38

Morris, Boris, Norris, and Floris

crawled out from under the bed.

39

"Eek! A witch!" yelled Norris.

"What have you done with Doris?"

asked Morris.

"The witch must have turned Doris
into this chair," said Norris.

"Poor Doris," cried Boris.

"I will never forget you.

Whenever I sit down,

I will think of you."

"Doris, can you hear me?"

Morris yelled.

"Yes," said Doris.

"I am so sad that the witch

turned me into a chair.

Now I will miss Halloween with you."

Doris took off her hat

and mask

and began to cry.

"Doris, you are not a chair!"

said Norris. "I am so happy!"

"I am happy, too," said Boris.

"But you would have been

a nice chair."

"Thank you for scaring

that witch away," said Morris.

"It was nothing," said Doris.

44

"What did you get for Halloween?"
asked Norris.

"Things for our party," said Doris.

"Hooray! We can celebrate,"
said Morris.

"And stay inside," said Boris.

So Boris, Morris, and Norris

got dressed up, too.

They ate candy.

Floris did her tricks.

And they had a very special
Know-Nothing Halloween party
.—even without Bob and the apples.